Pearl Harbor Is Burning!

THE EXCHANGE

What makes a good friend?

Pearl Harbor Is Burning!

A STORY OF WORLD WAR II

BY KATHLEEN V. KUDLINSKI

ILLUSTRATED BY RONALD HIMLER

 HAMPTON-BROWN

To Deborah Brodie,
gifted editor, valued friend

Many thanks to Sensei H. Tadao Imoto, Goju-Ryu Karate-do

Pearl Harbor Is Burning! written by Kathleen V. Kudlinski and illustrated by Ronald Himler. Text copyright © 1991 by Kathleen V. Kudlinski. Illustrations copyright © 1991 by Ronald Himler. Cover illustration © 1991 by Ronald Himler. Published by arrangement with Viking Children's Books, a division of Penguin Young Readers Group, a member of Penguin Group (USA) Inc.

On-Page Coach™ (introductions, questions, on-page glossaries), The Exchange, back cover summary © Hampton-Brown.

Hampton-Brown
P.O. Box 223220
Carmel, California 93922
800-333-3510
www.hampton-brown.com

Printed in the United States of America

ISBN-13: 978-0-7362-2779-7
ISBN-10: 0-7362-2779-2

06 07 08 09 10 11 12 13 14 10 9 8 7 6 5 4 3

Contents

Frank has just moved to Hawaii. He is not making friends. Then he meets Kenji. They both like baseball. They decide to meet on Sunday.

Aloha, Dummy

"Hey, you dumb **haoli**, you stop!"

Frank wanted to look back, to yell at the boy who was following him up the hill. But he knew better than to stop.

Why won't they leave me alone? Frank wondered. Dad had said that Hawaii was a friendly place. It wasn't that way for a fifth grade boy. Especially not a *haoli* from the **mainland**.

"*Hey, how-lee!*" The boy was by his elbow now. "You no can hear?"

Frank kept climbing the hill. He thought the boy was in his class at school, but he wasn't sure. He'd never been around so many Asians. It wasn't this way in Maryland. Two more island boys caught up with them. One bumped into Frank's shoulder.

....

haoli white kid (in Hawaiian)

mainland main part of the United States; land that is not an island

"You all leave me alone." Frank tried not to sound scared. He hurried across the road behind a pineapple truck. The boys followed. Frank walked faster, his leather shoes slipping in the sandy dirt. Why wouldn't his mother let him **go barefoot** like everybody else here?

They were almost running. One of the boys knocked against his arm. Frank twisted, trying to catch his books, but they slipped out of his hand and tumbled down the hill behind him. He stopped and glared at the boys.

*"**Aloha**, haoli"* one of them said, with a mean grin. Frank took a step back and ran into another boy.

"Ow!" one of them cried.

When Frank leaned over to see what had happened, somebody shoved him from behind and yelled, **"Have a nice trip, dummy!"** Frank fell in a crazy sort of somersault onto the road.

He could hear the boys laughing as he

....

go barefoot walk around without shoes

Aloha Hello (in Hawaiian)

"Have a nice trip, dummy!" "I'm going to push you and make you fall down, stupid boy!"

scrambled off the road. Another pineapple truck blew its horn. The boys ran into the bushes or on up the street. The truck **roared by** a few feet from Frank's face, spraying sandy red dirt into his eyes.

The stink of gas and pineapple on the dusty roadside made him want to choke. Sand burned in his eyes. *Don't rub them*, he kept telling himself. Instead he rubbed his knees. The shredded fabric of his pants was sticky with dirt and fresh blood.

"Hey, *haoli!*"

Frank shook his head and squinted into the tropical sun. Another boy walked over to him and held out his hand. Frank wiped tears off his cheeks, and with them, the last of the sand. This boy looked Asian, too.

Frank looked back up the sidewalk to see the gang running away. **"You one of them?"** Frank asked.

The boy shook his head, no. "I am Kenji. You need help to get books?" Frank reached for Kenji's hand and got to his feet. He groaned as his pants legs moved over his raw skin.

....

roared by loudly drove

"You one of them?" "Are you like those boys who hurt me?"

He looked straight at Kenji. "Hey, wait. You're in my class. Isn't your name George?"

The boy gave him a friendly grin. "That my English name. My school name. Everywhere else, I am Kenji."

"Does everyone have two names here?" Kenji nodded. That was why he hadn't been able to **figure out** who was in his class, Frank thought.

The boys began gathering the **scattered schoolwork**. It took a while. They found Frank's math paper in a flower bush. His reading book was on somebody's lawn. His spelling work had fresh tire tracks across the back.

"Those creeps could have killed me," he grumbled when he found his library book. Its cover, with the picture of Babe Ruth on it, was almost ripped off.

"No. They just **fooling around**. Bullies. They give every new *haoli* **a hard time** for a while." Kenji handed Frank his arithmetic book. "Those

---

figure out understand
scattered schoolwork school papers on the street
fooling around joking
a hard time trouble

guys study judo with me. If they wanted to, they would hurt you bad."

Frank wanted to ask what judo was. There certainly wasn't any of it in Maryland. But he didn't want to look stupid. Instead, he asked, "What kind of a name is Kenji?" as they gathered up the last of his books.

"Japanese."

"Swell! I've never known anybody from Japan."

"You dumb *haoli*. I was born in Hawaii. Me one American like you."

"Oh." Kenji didn't look or sound like any American Frank had ever known, but it wouldn't be polite to say so. "Well, uh, thanks for the help."

Frank grunted as the pile of books bumped into his sore ribs. He shifted them into his other arm, and began limping back up the hill. To his surprise, Kenji came along.

"You like baseball?" Kenji asked, pointing to the tattered library book Frank held.

"I pitch."

"You any good?"

Frank nodded. "**Our team was 12 and 0** last

....

Our team was 12 and 0 We won 12 games and lost 0 games

spring. Does Pearl City School have a team?"

"We were tops in 1941, too! Our best pitcher just moved off island. We sure can use you!"

That sounded great, Frank thought. Maybe Kenji could introduce him to some other team members. Ones he could really be friends with. For now at least he had somebody to talk to.

"You collect baseball cards?" he asked. When Kenji nodded, Frank grinned. "Do you **trade**? I have an extra 1937 Joe DiMaggio. Maybe we could throw a ball around, too." Frank stopped by the gate to his house. "Hey, you didn't have to walk me home."

"I live two doors down the street from you. My father owns your house."

Now Frank did feel dumb. "How come I never see you on the street?" he asked in surprise.

"I don't have much time. After school, I take classes in Japanese. Saturdays, I go to classes at the Japanese Community Center at the Buddhist temple."

"What about Sunday? I've got a **tree fort**

....

trade give and take baseball cards with other people

tree fort small room I made in a tree

down in the **gully** by Pearl Harbor. Want to play there in the morning?"

"*You* built that? I've seen it on my way home from the Center. It's swell!"

"We'd have to get there early," Frank said. "I have to be home and **cleaned up** in time for church."

"Is six too early?" Kenji asked. Frank shook his head, no. "Great. Don't forget your baseball cards!" Kenji waved and **headed down** the street.

Kenji could find me a friend, Frank thought. *After a month in Hawaii, I finally might meet a friend here.* He took a deep breath. "I *do* have friends," he said out loud. "Lots of them." Then, more quietly, "But they're all 10,000 miles away."

Frank walked slowly up the front steps. His mother wouldn't like Kenji at all. He knew what she'd say. "He's not the sort of boy your father and I want you to spend time with." Frank decided that he just wouldn't tell her about Kenji.

....

gully low land
cleaned up washed and dressed
headed down walked down

"Hurry, Franklin." She met him at the door. "I've finally found a nice friend for you. He's waiting inside." She looked out over his head. "And just who was that walking with you?"

BEFORE YOU MOVE ON...

1. **Conflict** The story started with a problem. What was it?

2. **Inference** Why did Frank think that Kenji was not American?

LOOK AHEAD Read pages 17–26 to meet Weston. Will he be a good friend for Frank?

Frank's mother invites a friend over for Frank. She thinks they will like each other. Frank is not so sure that they will have fun together.

Island Boy

"I'm waiting, young man." Frank's mother stood in the hallway, her hands on her hips. "Who was that boy?"

"His name is Kenji. He says his father owns this house."

"Oh. Yes." Mrs. Hopkins **paused**. "Well, do come in and meet Weston." She **glanced down** at his ripped pants. "Do I need to look at those knees?" Frank shook his head. Having a hospital nurse for a mother was great. When he really needed help, she knew just what to do. And she'd seen so much in the emergency room back home that she never got upset over little scrapes. "Go and change, then," she said. "Hurry now, you hear?"

....

paused stopped talking for a very short time
glanced down looked

Frank ran cold water on a washcloth and washed off the dried blood. When he looked into the mirror, he **scowled**. His normally blue eyes were red from the sand. Would Weston think he'd been crying? He splashed his face with cold water. More reddish dirt fell out of his hair. He hurried into a fresh pair of pants and joined his mother in the living room.

"Frank," his mother said, "this is Mrs. Griffith and Weston."

"I'm pleased to meet you, ma'am," Frank said, shaking her hand. He knew **he would be scolded later if he forgot his manners**. He turned to look into a pair of the palest blue eyes he had ever seen. "Pleased to meet you," he said to Weston. Frank could almost hear his mother smile.

"Why don't you boys **help yourselves to** a brownie and go out to play?" she suggested.

Frank led the way to the kitchen and poured two cups of milk. Weston helped himself to a brownie from a plate on the kitchen table, and

....

scowled made an angry face

he would be scolded later if he forgot his manners
his mother would be angry if he was not nice

help yourselves to take

asked, "Why are you living in Hawaii?"

"My father is a newspaper editor. He's here to work on the *Honolulu Star Bulletin*. He said we'd get to know the real Hawaii if we came for a year instead of just for a vacation."

"My father is a Navy doctor," Weston said, "so we get to live **on the base** with all the other Navy families. I go to school there." He had another brownie. "Are there real Hawaiians at your school?"

"Sure. And real Chinese." Frank grabbed a second brownie, too. "And real Japanese. And real Filipinos. And even a couple of other *haolis*."

"What's a *haoli*?"

"That's you and me. White kids from the mainland." Frank's knees were stinging. "They're not very friendly to *haolis* here."

"You should be on a military base. Most everybody is new, so everybody is friendly. And you don't have to **mix with the locals**."

Frank decided to ask his dad if they could move to the base, too.

....

on the base where the military works
mix with the locals see the Hawaiian people

"Did you leave us some brownies?" Mrs. Hopkins called from the living room. The boys quickly looked down at the plate. There were two pieces left. They grinned at each other and carried the plate in to serve their mothers.

"And, Margaret, you should see the strange foods they eat," Frank's mother was complaining. "It's almost impossible to make **a proper meal** here. And all these odd fruits!" Frank's mother threw up her hands.

Mrs. Griffith shook her head. "You should come shopping on the base with me. It's just like a store back home."

"Oh, could I? I miss the States **so**." Mrs. Hopkins seemed to remember the boys. "Why don't you two play outside now?" She turned to Weston's mother. "Frank hasn't found a single friend on his own here."

"I do too have a friend," Frank said quickly. "His name is Kenji. We're getting together Sunday morning."

"You told that boy you'd meet him?" Mrs.

....

a proper meal American food

so a lot

Hopkins's voice **was cool**. When Frank nodded, she said, "Well, Franklin, of course you must **follow through with your promise** and see him this once."

As soon as they were outside, Frank took a deep breath. The warm ocean breeze smelled good after the stuffy air in the living room. Most people in Hawaii, he had noticed, sat on their porches to enjoy the soft wind. They even ate supper in the shade of the porch roof. The Hopkins family had never tried that.

Frank picked up his mitt and tossed a ball to Weston. He missed it. "You need to warm up a bit?" Frank asked.

"No. I don't play baseball."

"You don't?" Frank was **stunned**. "What do you play?"

"I play chess. Do you?"

Frank shook his head. What was there to talk about? "I have a tree fort down in the gully. Want to see it?"

....

was cool sounded as if she did not like the idea

follow through with your promise do what you said you were going to do

stunned surprised

This time, Weston shook his head, no. "Too many bugs in those places. I guess we'll have to play ball."

No matter how easy Frank made his throws to Weston, his new friend couldn't catch them. "You want to practice your pitching instead?" Frank offered. Weston shrugged. "See the old tire under that tree? Try to throw the ball through it, like this."

Frank **wound up** and pitched the ball cleanly through the tire. He pointed to the mark by his toe. "From here to that tire is exactly how far it is from a pitcher's mound to home plate. I even hung the tire at just the right height for a fair pitch." Weston's face looked blank. "Just try it," Frank finally said.

Weston's first pitch flew over the tire. The next one was wide. Weston threw five more balls without **sending one** through the tire.

"I said chess is my game," he said **stiffly**.

Frank could feel how upset Weston was. "I've

....

wound up got ready to throw
sending one making the ball go
stiffly in an unfriendly way

never even tried chess," he offered. "Could you teach me some this afternoon?"

"I don't play much with beginners anymore."

"Boys!" Frank's mother called from the back door. "You all come in, now."

They walked silently to the door. "I've asked Weston and his mother to come back on Monday. Won't that be nice?"

Frank's father came home just as the guests were leaving. "I've heard a lot about your husband, Mrs. Griffith," he said. Weston grinned. Frank tried not to put weight on his sore knees.

It seemed forever before the Griffiths left. Finally Mrs. Hopkins started dinner and Frank and his father could go out to the backyard.

"Young Weston seems **a bit stiff**," Frank's father said, as they took turns pitching through the tire.

Frank grinned. "He doesn't like baseball, Dad. He isn't interested in my tree house. And he's scared of pineapple bugs." The balls **sailed** through the tire with a steady rhythm.

....

a bit stiff uncomfortable

sailed went easily

"There's nothing for Weston and me to talk about. And now I have to spend all Monday with him, too."

"Sometimes the best kind of friends are the ones who teach us new things."

"He won't," Frank said **sharply**.

"Won't what?"

"He said he wouldn't teach me chess."

"*I* can do that," Mr. Hopkins said. Frank looked at him in surprise. His father laughed and nodded. "It's been a long time since I played, but I still remember enough to teach you."

As they gathered the balls under the tree, Frank imagined how Weston's face would look if he **beat him at** chess on Monday. He looked up at the shiny red mountain apples. The other boys ate them. He picked one and took a bite. A starchy sweet taste filled his mouth.

Everything was perfect. The evening sun was warm, his arm muscles felt good from pitching just right, and his father was home. Hawaii wasn't so bad, after all.

....

sharply with anger
beat him at won the game of

"Frank," Mr. Hopkins said. "Are you sure that fruit is safe?"

"It no can hurt you," Frank said. His father laughed loud and long before Frank realized what he had said. He blushed. "I mean it can't hurt you."

"My island boy." Mr. Hopkins put his arm around Frank and walked him into the house. "Martha, your boy is eating island fruit and speaking **Pidgin English** already. He'll be a **native** before we know it."

"Not in my house," she said sharply. "Now, wash up for dinner."

....

Pidgin English Hawaiian English
native Hawaiian

BEFORE YOU MOVE ON...

1. **Conflict** Weston and Frank did not become good friends. Why?

2. **Character** How can you tell that Frank's mom did not trust people who were not like her?

LOOK AHEAD Read pages 27–31 to find out if Frank and Kenji like each other.

Frank and Kenji meet on Sunday. They eat breakfast and play ball. Suddenly their fun ends. Japanese airplanes bomb Pearl Harbor.

Attack!

Frank was **panting** by the time he reached his tree fort. He unzipped his Baltimore Orioles jacket. It would never be this warm at home on December 7, he thought. "Kenji?" he called. "You here yet?"

"**Eyes up!**" Kenji yelled from above his head. "**Pop fly headed for** center field!" Frank saw only a flash as Kenji tossed a ball at him from the fort.

Without thinking, Frank cupped his hands. He found the ball against the silvery banyan leaves, and caught it easily.

He threw it back at Kenji. "You're out!" he yelled.

"Swell catch!" Kenji grinned at him over the driftwood railing. "Hey, I wait half-hour for you. I thought you no come, it got so late."

---

panting breathing hard
Eyes up! Look up here!
Pop fly headed for A high ball is going toward

"My mom didn't make it easy," Frank said. "Oops—she no make it easy," he corrected himself.

"Hey, *haoli*, you no have to talk Pidgin with me. I know English from school. Besides, all kids talk Pidgin when they stay in Hawaii. You don't have to try. It just happen."

"Where does Pidgin English come from?" Frank asked. It wasn't anything he'd ever heard about before he came to Hawaii.

"All kind of kids from all over the world come to islands. Or maybe all kind of men. Nobody talk the same, but they want to be friends." Kenji moved over to make room as Frank climbed up onto the tree-house floor beside him. "So they make their own way of talking, with words from all their homes. Hey, this is **some fort**!"

Frank looked around with pride. The tree house **sagged** on one side, but it was **lashed tight** with rope he'd found on the beach. Tides had brought him every piece of driftwood he had used, too, and

....

some fort a nice fort
sagged leaned; was not straight
lashed tight tied tightly

every old crate and colorful fishing float. He had gathered it, day by day. Then he carried it all up the hill through soggy, shoulder-high ferns. Finally, he had pulled each piece up into the tree and lashed it into place.

"But *that's* the best part," Frank said, waving at the view over Pearl Harbor. "**The whole Pacific fleet is here**. Dad said there are more than 90 Navy ships in the **harbor** right now."

He put his hand in a pocket. "Say, I brought some ham biscuits for breakfast. Want one?"

Kenji reached into his own pocket. "I bring something for you, too," he said with a grin. "You ever try rice balls?"

The boys traded, and Frank saw that Kenji was watching him closely. "Thanks," he said and bit deeply into the fist-sized ball of rice. **His face puckered** as the rice ball fell apart in his mouth. Something horribly sour and salty was hidden in the ball. He'd been tricked!

....

The whole Pacific fleet is here. All of the American ships in the Pacific Ocean are here.

harbor water where boats come to land

His face puckered He looked like he ate something bad

Frank wanted to spit it out, but Kenji was still grinning, so he chewed, instead. The flavors melted together and the taste changed. It was a little sweet, too, Frank realized. He swallowed hard, and made himself smile back at Kenji. Why hadn't he brought a canteen of water with him? He stuffed the other half of the rice ball in his mouth.

Without the surprise this time, Frank enjoyed the strong sharp flavor hidden inside the rice. It was still a strange taste, but good.

"You like?" Kenji asked. "I've got more." They shared the rest of their breakfasts, looking out over the harbor.

The rising sun **gleamed** on the smokestacks of huge battleships tied to concrete pilings off Ford Island. It looked like a whole city of war, its skyscrapers **bristling with** guns and gangways, flags and conning towers.

"The farthest one from here is the *Maryland*," Frank pointed out proudly. "That's where I live. Or lived. Well, Maryland is where I'm going back to next year." They looked out at the battleship

---

gleamed shined
bristling with full of

together. "Dad got me a map of the ships so I could pick her out. Those over there are destroyers. The little ones are cruisers."

"Little?" Kenji asked, and they both laughed. The cruisers were enormous, even at this distance.

"Hey, did you bring your baseball cards?"

Kenji grinned. "Of course." As they dug into their pockets, a buzzing sound filled the sky. Kenji didn't even look up. "There they are again. Practice raids. Sometimes all the planes make my mother's head hurt."

Frank suddenly wondered about Kenji's family. What was a Japanese mother like? A Japanese-American mother, he corrected himself. Would she wear a kimono or a housedress? Did Kenji's father ever pitch balls?

BEFORE YOU MOVE ON...

1. **Character** Did it seem like Frank and Kenji would be friends? How did you know?

2. **Plot** Reread pages 30 and 31. How can you tell a war was starting?

LOOK AHEAD Read pages 32–39 to find out what surprises the boys see in the sky.

A deep thumping sound reached them across the water, and both boys turned to see a dark plane **heading right for** them. As it pulled up to **clear the hillside**, they could see a bright red ball painted on its side.

"It's a Japanese plane!" Kenji screamed into the roar of its engines.

"They're bombing Hickham Field!" Frank shouted. Both boys stood to get a view of the far airstrip. Giant black clouds bloomed, blew away with the wind, and bloomed again. The low thumping of each explosion rolled slowly across the water. Flames soared over the Army aircraft parked on the ground.

Japanese planes swooped overhead from every direction. Frank had never seen so many planes in the sky at once. It was beautiful. Exciting. Loud. But it couldn't be real. It looked like the Fourth of July and an old war movie **all rolled together**. While he held his ears against the roar, Frank saw a plane drop a bomb into the water.

....

heading right for coming toward
clear the hillside fly over the hill
all rolled together at the same time

Bombing the water? he wondered. Then he realized what he'd seen. "A **torpedo**!" he cried.

A cruiser exploded into a red burst of flame. Now oily black smoke was billowing all around Pearl Harbor. Air raid sirens began to scream from every ship.

"Here come some more!" yelled Kenji. These planes were flying so low that the wind from their propellers whipped the water into whitecaps. And they were heading straight toward the battleships. The boys saw them drop torpedo after torpedo, before they pulled up at the last minute to roar away into the sky.

"That's the *Oklahoma!*" Frank shouted as the first big battleship took a hit. "There goes the *West Virginia!*"

"Jeez! Look at that one!" Kenji cried over the **thundering drone** of hundreds of airplanes.

"That's the *Arizona!*" Frank yelled, watching the ship burst into flame. "And they got it again!" Oil slicks flooding across the water were on fire.

"No! No!" Frank and Kenji shrieked. They

....

torpedo bomb that explodes underwater
thundering drone noisy sound

stamped their feet as another battleship took a double hit. They had to grab a branch as some of Frank's carefully tied knots slipped. "That was the *California!*" he shouted.

"It almost got *us*, too!" Kenji laughed nervously as the tree fort **settled to a sharper tilt**. "Oh, look!"

A Japanese plane tumbled into the harbor below the fort. "Hooray!" Both boys recklessly stamped their feet again.

Now **anti-aircraft fire** began exploding in puffs of black smoke. "Get him! Get him!" They cheered the U.S. Navy on.

An explosion tore apart the corner of the nearest destroyer. For the first time, the boys could see tiny figures running to and fro on the burning ship. "The *Nevada*," Frank said, but the **glee** had gone out of his voice.

Choking smoke blew past the boys, bringing with it the faint sound of men screaming. They watched in horror as the giant *West Virginia* slowly

....

settled to a sharper tilt fell more
anti-aircraft fire gunshots from the Navy fighting back
glee happiness

sank to the shallow bottom of the harbor, sending waves crashing against the beach below them.

Two more bombs exploded on the *Arizona*. Then the *Oklahoma* started to roll. The whole ship slowly turned over and settled into the mud. **It was too real now.** Frank didn't want to see any more, but he couldn't look away.

The harbor was full of sirens and smoke and men **scrambling** for safety. Suddenly a blinding light flashed across the water. The *Arizona* exploded in a huge ball of flame that filled the sky and sent shock waves to sweep men off the decks of all the nearby ships. When the sound hit Frank, he thought his ears would burst. There couldn't be anything left of that ship, he thought.

And still the planes kept coming. Bombs dropped until the air was one steady sound of explosion, drowning out the roar of the planes.

When the attack ended, the boys stood silently. Finally, Frank wiped his eyes and began picking up the scattered baseball cards. His ears still rang.

....

It was too real now. Frank realized the attack was real.
scrambling running

His mind was numb. He glanced at his watch. The whole attack had taken less than half an hour!

Out in the harbor, ship engines **began rumbling**. Some raced to help other ships or to rescue men from the burning waters. A few headed out to sea. The huge *Nevada* slowly pulled away from Ford Island, heading for the open ocean, her gun barrels pointed skyward.

"Oh, no!" Frank moaned, as the sky filled again. The Japanese were back with a second attack. It wasn't fair! But this time, Frank and Kenji cheered. Now the U.S. Navy was fighting back. **Shells streaked upward** from every ship that could fire at the planes. Even those ships pulled up out of the water for repairs were fighting this attack.

More destroyers and cruisers were hit; **more were sunk**. Finally, with one last shattering explosion, the sky was clear again.

....

His mind was numb. He couldn't think anymore.

began rumbling started up

Shells streaked upward Large bullets went up

more were sunk many ships were destroyed and went underwater

"Will they be back?" Kenji **wondered over the sounds of sirens**.

"I don't know," Frank answered, looking at the smoke-filled harbor. "But we have to do something to help!"

....

wondered over the sounds of sirens asked as he listened to the sirens

BEFORE YOU MOVE ON...

1. **Conclusions** Reread page 34. What showed you that Frank and Kenji were surprised by the bombing?

2. **Cause and Effect** Reread page 35. What happened that made Kenji and Frank cheer?

LOOK AHEAD Read pages 40–50 to find out why the principal went to school on a Sunday.

Kenji and Frank help put tape on the windows at the school. The tape will stop the windows from breaking if there is more bombing.

The Race

"You go to help, Frank. I go home."

Frank looked at Kenji. "You've got to be kidding! What are you—scared?"

"A son's first duty is to his family." The way Kenji said it made Frank think of the **Ten Commandments**. It also made him think of his own mother. She would be worried.

"Oh . . ." He started to argue, but Kenji was already climbing down the rope ladder. Frank looked back at the smoke-filled harbor. **Sirens wailed** from every direction. "Wait up, Kenji!" he called.

....

"A son's first duty is to his family." "I need to help my family first."

Ten Commandments rules in the Bible

Sirens wailed Alarms made loud sounds

They scrambled through the ferns and vines together. A police car roared past, sending a cloud of powdery white sand into their faces. Another police car followed, siren blasting, and then another.

"Come on, let's go!" Frank shouted and started running up the road toward home.

They slowed down near a house where **the sound of a radio floated out over the road**. "Do not **panic**," the announcer was saying. "We repeat. There is no cause for panic. The Japanese attack appears to be over." Kenji and Frank looked at each other and grinned with relief.

"Wait. Someone just brought in a note," the radio voice went on. "It says that a Japanese ship has landed at the north end of the island. If anyone knows more, please call the station. And, remember, keep off the roads so emergency vehicles can get through."

The Glenn Miller Band came on. Frank and Kenji sang along as they walked away. Before they

....

the sound of the radio floated out over the road they heard the radio inside

panic get scared or nervous

finished the first line, the song stopped. "There *is* no Japanese ship," the radio speaker called out. "Repeat. There is *no* ship. A listener with a good view of the north end called in. I guess all it is safe to say is that **rumors are sweeping the island**. Just remember, don't panic. We will bring you news as it **breaks**." And the band was back, playing a love song.

Four army trucks rushed by in a row, stirring up more sand. A blue car hurried after them, then took a turn and **squealed** down the school's driveway. "Hey, wasn't that Mr. Marsh?" Frank asked.

"Why would the principal go to school Sunday morning?" Kenji wondered aloud.

"Let's go see," Frank said. "It won't take much time. Then we'll go right home." They turned into the driveway.

"Boys, am I ever glad to see you!" called Mr. Marsh. "This school is going to be used for emergency meetings today. We have to tape the

....

rumors are sweeping the island people are telling stories that may not be true

breaks happens

squealed made a loud noise as it drove

windows. That way, if there's another bombing run, the glass won't break into **splinters** on the people inside." He held out two big rolls of tape. "Here, Frank." *He already knows my name!* Frank thought, happily.

"This is yours, George." Frank looked at Kenji. What would it be like to have two names? Frank was glad he knew Kenji's real name.

"Come on now, boys." Kenji wouldn't take the tape, and Frank didn't want to if Kenji didn't. He knew his mother would be worried. But she'd want him to **obey** the principal, too. And they'd be doing something to help!

He grabbed both rolls and handed one to Kenji. "I'll race you!" he teased. "Let's start by the front door. I'll go after the windows to the left, you take the right, and we race to the playground door in back."

Kenji shook his head, no.

"*Then* we'll go home, I promise," Frank said. Kenji took the tape.

"Good," Mr. Marsh said. "You can stand on

---

splinters pieces
obey listen to

those pineapple crates. I'll tape the second floor windows from inside." He ran and got pails of water for each of them. "Ready? Set? Go!"

Frank grabbed his pineapple crate and **set it up** beside the building. He knew what to do. He had taped the windows at home in Maryland once when a hurricane was coming. He dipped the tape into water, then stretched up on his toes and stuck the end of the tape to one corner of the glass. Then he unrolled it to the far bottom corner, pressing it into place as he went. Then dip and up again to make a giant X.

By the time he turned the corner of the building, **the motions had settled into a pattern**. Dip. Up. Down. Dip. Up. Down. Move over to the next window, and dip again. He wondered how far Kenji had gotten. The long side of the building seemed to be going on forever. He tried to remember if there would be two or three windows left when he finally turned the next corner.

....

set it up put it

the motions had settled into a pattern he really knew what he was doing

When **his mind wandered**, he saw the men blown off the deck of the *Arizona*. Torpedos churning through the water toward ships tied helplessly at anchor. Flames burning on decks. On piers. On oil slicks. The water itself had seemed on fire. Frank tried to move even faster, to **rip the memories out** as he ripped the tape off its roll.

At least Kenji had been there to see it with him. It would have been too awful to watch the bombing alone. Kenji was fun to **pal around** with, Frank thought. At least until he found a real friend. Besides, Kenji wasn't so strange, after all. He was just like anybody else on the baseball team back home. Almost. He began to whistle "Take Me Out to the Ball Game." Finally he **rounded** the corner and set his crate under the next-to-last window.

"Hey, *haoli*, I'm out of tape," Kenji called from the top of his crate. "Let's see your fastball." He cupped his hands, squatted into a catcher's stance, and almost fell off the crate. Kenji laughed at

....

his mind wandered he thought about the bombing

rip the memories out forget the memories of the attack

pal around play

rounded turned

himself, and Frank hurled the tape squarely into his hands.

"Nice catch," Frank called. It would be great to be on a team with Kenji, he thought.

They were finished in minutes. A block and a half from home, a police car stopped beside them. "You boys," the officer said. "Where are you going?"

"Home," Frank answered.

The officer looked closely at Kenji. "Who are *you*?" he demanded.

"George Imoto, sir," Kenji answered. The policeman kept studying him. "I no live two blocks from here."

"His daddy owns the house where we're staying," Frank put in. The officer wrote both of their names down and told them to hurry home.

When they got to Frank's house, Kenji waved a quick good-bye and kept walking.

"Mom! I'm home!" Frank called as he opened the door. His mother **darted out from** the kitchen and grabbed him in a long, fierce hug.

....

darted out from walked quickly out of

"Frank, oh, my Frank," she kept saying. When he could pull away, he saw she'd been crying. "I've been so scared. Your father waited as long as he could for you, but he was needed at the newspaper." She sighed. "They've attacked, Frank. While you were out playing, the Japanese bombed everything."

"Not everything, Mom," Frank said. "Some of the ships are still floating."

"How do you know this?" she asked sharply.

"I saw it." Frank shook his head, trying to **keep out the pictures**. "Kenji and I watched it all. The bombs and the fires and the torpedos. And, Mom, they hit the *Maryland!*"

"Attention, please." The radio voice **burst out** from the kitchen. "Private citizens are to prepare their homes **for blackout conditions** tonight. Stay tuned to this band for further announcements." And as suddenly as it had begun, the radio news was over.

....

keep out the pictures not think about the attack
burst out spoke
for blackout conditions and make sure there are no lights on

"We have to talk about tonight, Frank," Mrs. Hopkins said. He followed her to the kitchen. "They called for all nurses to **report** to their nearest hospital to help with wounded soldiers." She handed him a sandwich.

"Are you going?"

"Of course. I have to do something to help!"

Frank smiled. He knew that feeling. "Swell!" he said. While she poured milk for him, he told about helping at the school on the way home. Then he told her about the policeman stopping them and writing down his name.

"Oh, dear." His mother looked out the window. "I wish you had found a **safer friend**." He knew what she meant. Safe and white. But there were only two other white kids in his class and both of them were girls. All the rest were Japanese, or Chinese, or Korean, or Hawaiian. Why couldn't his mother understand? That was how it *was* in Hawaii!

....

report go
safer friend friend who isn't Japanese American

"Kenji Imoto is just like me, Mom. You should see how he can catch!"

"Well, I hope, so, Franklin. **It would fit right in with** the plans your father made for you." She gave her white uniform a sharp tug. "While I'm at the hospital, you will be spending the night at the Imotos' with that Kenji."

....

It would fit right in with Kenji is a part of

BEFORE YOU MOVE ON...

1. **Character's Motive** The school was open to hold emergency meetings. Why did Kenji not want to help at the school at first?

2. **Character's Point of View** Reread page 49. What did Frank wish his mother would understand?

LOOK AHEAD Read pages 51–57 to find out what surprises Frank about a Japanese home.

Many people are hurt from the bombing. Frank's mother goes to the hospital. Frank goes to Kenji's house. It is a traditional Japanese home.

Chopsticks

Frank looked at the pairs of sandals **lined up neatly** outside the Imotos' door. "Mom!" he whispered. "Look where they keep their shoes!" There were tiny sandals, large red sandals, and black ones, too. At the end of the row sat a pair of brown men's shoes and a pair of tennis shoes Frank's size. He looked at his own shoes, covered with red dust. "Should I take mine off, too?"

"Oh, dear," Mrs. Hopkins said, "I don't know. No. That wouldn't be **good manners**." Then she looked at the lines of shoes waiting on both sides of the door and sighed. "Yes, but *hurry*." She pushed the doorbell.

Frank bent to untie his shoelaces. The door opened, and Frank found himself looking at a pair

....

lined up neatly in a row
good manners correct, nice

of lady's bare feet. "Welcome," a soft voice said over his head.

"My name is Joyce Hopkins," Frank's mother introduced herself. She grabbed Frank's collar and pulled up on it. "And this is Franklin."

"I'm pleased to meet you, ma'am," Frank said to the feet. He struggled to stand up and put out his hand to shake, but Mrs. Imoto was **bowing**. Frank stood in amazement, one hand out and one shoe off. No one had ever bowed to him. Should he bow back?

He looked to see what his mother was doing about it. She bowed quickly to Kenji's mother, so Frank did, too. "Will you come in for tea?" Mrs. Imoto's **accent** made it hard for Frank to understand what she was saying.

"No, thank you," his mother answered. "I have to get to the hospital." Frank could hear the relief in his mother's voice. "But thank you so much for keeping Franklin tonight."

....

bowing bending over a little
accent way of speaking English

"**It is an honor** to help you to help our poor boys." Frank looked from Mrs. Imoto to his mother. One was standing in a kimono and bare feet, the other in a nurse's white uniform and oxford shoes. *Our* boys? "Go then. I will care for Frank-*chan*." Frank Chan? Hadn't she heard his last name right? How could he tell her without being rude? Mrs. Imoto was bowing again as Frank's mother left.

"*Mah!* So many dead! So many hurt!" Mrs. Imoto said, and shook her head and sighed. "I will get Kenji-*chan*." *Kenji-chan*? The way she said it sounded nice, whatever it meant. Frank knelt to untie his other shoe.

"*Aloha*." Now Frank was looking at Kenji's **stocking feet**. "Did you bring your baseball cards?"

Frank pulled the cards from his jacket pocket and grinned. "You bet." He followed Kenji indoors and looked around. The living room was almost empty. No chairs. No rug. One low square table in

---

It is an honor I am happy
stocking feet feet without shoes

the middle of the room. "Did you just **move in**?"
he asked.

"No. Grandfather took the house when he
came from Japan to cut sugarcane. My father was
born here. Me, too."

"Come, put your things in my room," Kenji said.
Frank followed him down a hall. Two flags stood
in a vase as if they were flowers. One showed the
Stars and Stripes. The other had the same rising
sun that had glared at Frank from hundreds of
bombers just hours ago. He stopped to stare, then
had to hurry to follow Kenji into his room.

"Where's the bed? And your desk?" Kenji's
bedroom was even worse than the living room.
There was nothing but a wide wooden shelf
around the wall. "Where do you keep your
clothes? Why is everything white?"

Kenji laughed as Frank looked around. "What is
wrong with you, *haoli*? You never see a Japanese
house?" Frank shook his head. "Give me your
jacket." Kenji opened a door that was under the
shelf and hung Frank's jacket on a hook inside.

move in start living here
Stars and Stripes American flag

Now Frank could see hidden doors all the way around the room.

There was one picture of mountains on the wall. A vase with just three flowers and a twisty leaf in it sat on the shelf. Nothing else.

Kenji opened another door and took his baseball cards off a shelf. "Let's see your Brooklyn Dodgers." He knelt on the floor and began laying his cards out in rows. "Wasn't that some pennant race?"

Frank sat down beside him and pulled out his own Dodgers. He decided to take out the Baltimore Orioles cards, too. Now he felt **at home**.

"Can you believe that Ted Williams?" Kenji asked. "Batting .406 in his second year in **the majors**?"

"Yeah. Remember the All-Star Game? Bottom of the ninth, the team down 5–4, Williams hits a **homer and drives in two**. What a swell play!"

"You know who I'd like to meet?" Kenji asked. Frank shook his head. "Joe DiMaggio."

---

at home comfortable

the majors major league baseball

homer and drives in two homerun and scores two points

Frank pulled out his card. "Hits in 56 straight games. That's some record!"

"I bet the **whole '41 season goes down in the history books**."

....

whole '41 season goes down in the history books year of 1941 baseball will be remembered for a long time

---

BEFORE YOU MOVE ON...

1. **Comparisons** Frank was surprised that the Imotos didn't wear shoes in the house like his family. What else is different from his home?

2. **Character** Why do you think Frank's mother was relieved she couldn't stay at the Imotos' house for tea?

LOOK AHEAD Read pages 58–63 to find out how Frank feels about his first Japanese dinner.

"Come. Eat." Mrs. Imoto's voice called them to the living room. The low table in the living room was set with plates and another nearly empty flower vase. No forks. No glasses. And still no chairs.

But there sure were a lot of people, Frank thought. He bowed to Kenji's grandfather and grandmother first. Then to his father. Next, he bowed to an aunt. Finally, he bowed to two younger sisters, Hanako and Emiko. Then it was time to eat.

"Sit here." Kenji patted a cushion on the floor and Frank quickly sat down beside him. Kenji's grandfather was the last in place, settling himself down to the floor slowly and **stiffly**. Sitting on the floor felt strange to Frank, but it did make the table the right height. Mrs. Imoto opened a big kettle and a spicy smell filled the room. The girls passed out bowls of steaming soup.

Dinner at home with his mom and dad was so quiet and polite. Here dinner was loud and friendly. Nine people talking in three different languages.

....

stiffly as if he could not bend easily

Whenever something was said to him in Pidgin or when he spoke in English, it had to be said again in Japanese for the grandparents. It got quiet every time Grandfather spoke, but **chatter burst out** again whenever he finished. The noise and the warmth **swirled** around Frank, as strange and delicious as the soup.

After the spoons and bowls were taken away, Mrs. Imoto brought a big bowl of rice and a plate of fish from the kitchen. There were funny-looking vegetables and a dish of pickles, too. It all smelled as good as the soup, but there was nothing to eat it with.

Kenji waved two sticks at him and grinned. "Chopsticks." He pointed to another pair of sticks lying above Frank's plate.

"You eat with sticks?" He watched Kenji grab a bite of fish with the chopsticks, and pop it into his mouth. Frank looked around the table. They were all using sticks. Hanako and Emiko were staring at him as they ate.

"Try," Kenji said.

....

chatter burst out people started talking
swirled was all

Frank did try. He dropped his rice on the table. Kenji's sisters giggled and Frank felt his face turn red. He tried again. The rice dropped on his lap. It just wasn't possible. And now all the Imotos were watching him.

Grandfather **eased himself up from his place**. He took Frank's hand and made him hold the chopsticks in a different way. Grandfather pointed at the fish, and Frank tried again. This time he got most of it into his mouth.

Hanako and Emiko clapped. Kenji cheered. **The table filled with chatter** again. "Frank-*chan*," Grandfather said and patted his shoulder.

After dinner, Mr. Imoto began talking to the family in Japanese. Kenji told Frank what he was saying. "There is a blackout tonight. A bomber **could use any lights for a target**," Kenji explained quietly while his father talked. "No lights can show through the windows. No flashlights. No car lights. Not even cigarettes!" Kenji grinned.

---

eased himself up from his place stood up slowly
The table filled with chatter Everyone started talking
could use any lights for a target might shoot at us if they see lights

His father's voice got even more serious. "No talking in Japanese out of the house," Kenji repeated for Frank. "No more Japanese flags."

"*Mah!*" Grandfather shouted. The Imoto men argued loudly while all the others looked at their plates.

"What's he saying?" Frank whispered again and again. Kenji just shook his head.

Before it got dark, they pasted tape strips on the windows of the Imoto house. Then the boys walked down to Frank's house and taped those windows, too. Kenji was quiet.

"What were your father and grandfather saying?" Frank tried again.

"We have to be careful," Kenji said.

"We do?"

"Not you. Us." Kenji sounded angry.

"Why?"

"They might attack us, Frank. Or put us in jail. All right?"

"Who? The Japanese?" Frank was confused.

"You, dummy," Kenji **muttered** and turned to go home. "The *haolis*."

---

muttered said quietly

BEFORE YOU MOVE ON...

1. **Character** Frank said that dinner was "loud and friendly" and "strange and delicious." What does this show about Frank?

2. **Conflict** Reread page 62. Why did Mr. Imoto say "no more talking in Japanese" and "no more Japanese flags"?

LOOK AHEAD Read pages 64–73 to find out what dangerous mistake Frank and Kenji make.

Frank and Kenji learn that the attacks are serious.
Frank is comfortable at his new friend's house.
Will there be more visits?

Air Raid

"Do we *have* to go to bed now?" Emiko was asking her mother when Frank and Kenji came in the door.

"We have no black shades to cover the windows, Emi-*chan*," Mrs. Imoto said. "We must turn out all the lights at dark. You have to be ready."

Frank followed Kenji back to his empty white bedroom. The Japanese flag was gone from the hall. Someone had pinned the American flag out against the wall to look like it was **waving** in a wind. Or, Frank thought, to cover the empty space beside it.

"So where do we sleep?" Frank finally asked.

Kenji grinned. "On *futons*. Watch." He pulled a straw mat from behind another door and spread

....

waving moving
futons Japanese beds

it on the floor. Then he took out a thick pad and a blanket and put them on top of the mat. Frank made a bed for himself the same way. He looked at it for a moment, then slid it across the floor to be nearer to Kenji. They could talk in a blackout, even if they couldn't keep the lights on. "How can you sleep on the floor?" he had to ask.

"How you sleep on a bed?" Kenji's answer was no answer at all. "Beds are too soft," he explained. "They bounce. You can fall out, get hurt. I no can sleep on bed."

It still sounded strange, Frank thought, looking down at his *futon*. "What about pillows?" he asked.

Kenji grabbed two small sacks from the top shelf and tossed them onto the *futons*. "But those are beanbags!" Frank **gasped**.

Kenji shrugged and lay down on the bed he'd made for himself on the floor. A **faint glow** from the sunset came through the window shades. In the dim light, Frank watched Kenji **settle** his head on the beanbag.

....

gasped said with surprise
faint glow a little light
settle put

He looked around the room. *There is no way I can sleep here*, Frank thought. *The house is full of strangers. And strange things.*

"Come on, *haoli*," Kenji said at last. "Try it." The way he said *haoli* made Frank smile. Kenji gave the word the same warm sound that Frank's teammates had back in Maryland when they talked to him.

Frank tried to make his head comfortable on the beanbag. The beans inside **shifted and rattled** loudly in his ear, so he stopped **squirming**.

"Kenji?" he asked into the darkness. "What does it mean when your mother calls me 'Frank-chan'?"

"It means she likes you. *O-yasumi nasai, haoli.*"

"What!?"

"*O-yasumi nasai* means good night."

"*O-yasumi nasai*, Kenji."

A screaming siren made Frank jump from his sleep. Where was he? What was the siren? Where was his mother? Everything was wrong.

....

shifted and rattled moved and made noise
squirming moving

He tried to get out of bed, but the floor was right there where air should be. The window was on the wrong side.

The door opened. The light of a small candle lit Mrs. Imoto's face. Frank relaxed. That explained where he was. But what was all the noise?

The siren wailed on and on. Mrs. Imoto came close and bent down between the two boys. "It is an air raid," she said loudly. Frank could barely hear her. "I do not think **there are planes in attack**. I have radio on. I will let you know." And she was gone.

And, suddenly, the siren was gone, too. **The silence was huge.** Frank listened hard for any sound. Had he lost his hearing?

"Just a test," Mrs. Imoto called from the hallway. "No danger. *O-yasumi nasai.*" And Frank could hear her footsteps padding away down the hall.

"Kenji? Can you get back to sleep?"

"No. You?"

....

there are planes in attack we are being attacked
The silence was huge. It was very quiet.

"**No chance**," Frank said. "You want to go outside and look at the blackout?"

There was a long silence. They shouldn't go out. Frank knew it. They could get into a lot of trouble. Kenji would say no, and that would end the whole crazy idea.

"Yes."

"What!" Frank said.

"You no can hear? Let's go."

They slipped through the back door and out into a moonless night.

Stars were everywhere across the sky. Their faint, blue light fell on the houses, the trees, the roads, and the bushes. Frank took a deep breath. The air was full of the strong sweet smell of night flowers. Tree frogs called from every bush.

"Come on!" Frank whispered. He wanted to see his own home in this spooky light. Frank led the way to the road.

"Halt!" A man's voice barked from behind them.

....

No chance No, I cannot

"Halt!" "Stop!"

Both boys ran. They fled straight down the sidewalk, away from the voice, but not away from the footsteps. The man was running, too, and his legs were longer. They could hear him catch up.

"Stop, you stupid kids," he panted from right behind them. They did. They couldn't get away. Frank turned to stand beside Kenji. Standing outdoors, barefoot and in his pajamas, Frank felt **almost naked**.

The starlight glittered on—a gun? He started running again, but the man grabbed his arm.

"What do you **clowns** think this is?" the man asked angrily. "A *game*? We're at war! I'm supposed to shoot anybody who doesn't stop when I call 'halt.'" He shook Frank's arm. "I could have shot you."

"And *you*." He looked at Kenji's face. "You stay indoors. The way people are feeling tonight, you might be shot as a spy whether you stopped or not."

....

almost naked like he had no clothes on
clowns stupid kids

"Now, let's walk on home." The man headed back up the sidewalk. Frank and Kenji **dragged on** behind him. The adventure was over.

Frank looked at the gun on the man's shoulder. He was keeping his hand against it as they walked. Frank wondered if that was to keep it quiet. Or to keep it ready. "You going to tell our folks?" he whispered.

"Naw. I got a boy like you. He'd want to be out tonight, too," the man said. Then he growled, "But he better not be!"

"Halt!" another voice called from up the street. "Who goes there?"

"It's me, Will. **All clear.**"

Frank and Kenji followed silently to the Imoto house. "I live here, sir," Kenji whispered.

"Then *stay* there!" He ruffled Kenji's hair before he strode on into the darkness.

Frank got back into bed, and watched as **slivers of dawn** slowly began to glow around the window shade. The Imoto house was very strange,

....

dragged on walked slowly

All clear. Everything is fine now.

slivers of dawn the sun

he thought, but it was peaceful. Quiet. Safe. It was nice to think that no matter what happened with the war, here he would be Frank-*chan*.

Kenji was already sleeping, his head resting on the beanbag. Frank had one more question to ask, but it could wait. First thing in the morning he would ask Kenji how to say "friend" in Japanese. Frank smiled and fell asleep.

BEFORE YOU MOVE ON...

1. **Cause and Effect** Frank and Kenji went outside to see the blackout. Why was this so dangerous?

2. **Inference** Reread page 72. How does Frank feel about Kenji? How do you know?

LOOK AHEAD Read some real facts about the war on pages 74–76.

The author made up Frank and Kenji. But the events really happened. To write this book, the author talked to people from Hawaii and did research.

About This Book

The bombing of Pearl Harbor happened just as I described it. The Japanese planned their surprise attack for early Sunday morning, December 7, 1941. They knew many **servicemen** would be away from their posts and the Hawaiians would just be getting out of bed.

In less than two hours of bombing, 2,300 Americans died, 960 were lost, and 1,100 more were wounded. Eight battleships lay sunk in Pearl Harbor, along with three cruisers, three destroyers, and three other ships. Japan was trying to destroy America's power in the Pacific so they could **take over**. Their plan didn't work.

....

servicemen men in the military
take over have all the power; control

The Japanese did not bomb Pearl Harbor's huge oil tanks, their **ammunition storage buildings**, or the U.S. submarines. They missed three aircraft carriers which were out at sea. They did not ruin the ship repair docks. Within six months, our Pacific fleet was stronger than it had ever been— and it went on to win the war that started in Pearl Harbor.

I made up Frank and Kenji and their story at Pearl Harbor. To make it realistic, I looked in old guide-books and talked to people who'd been in Hawaii 50 years ago. Then I spoke with my son Hal's karate teacher, a Japanese-American named Harry Tadao Imoto.

It was as if I had met **the real-life Kenji**. Not only had Tadao lived in Hawaii as a child, but he actually watched the bombing of Pearl Harbor (though he stood on top of a pigeon coop, not a tree fort). He remembered how some of the island children used to tease *haolis*. He said that he used

....

ammunition storage buildings buildings where they kept guns, bullets, bombs

the real-life Kenji someone just like Kenji

to feel sorry for the newcomers, and tried to make friends with them instead.

The true story took a cruel turn after the bombing. Thousands of Japanese-Americans were arrested as spies. Whole families were taken from their homes on the mainland. They were sent to live in vast prisons called internment camps. In Hawaii it was different.

Hawaiians are a mix of native islanders, Caucasians, Asian-Americans, and other groups. All of them work together to run the shops and farms, the schools and towns of the islands. Japanese-Americans were not the enemy in World War II. The islanders knew that from working side by side with them. There were a few arrests, but there were no internment camps in Hawaii.

K.V.K.

BEFORE YOU MOVE ON...

1. **Author's Point of View** Did the author feel her book was realistic? Why or why not?

2. **Cause and Effect** What happened to many Japanese Americans after the bombings of Pearl Harbor?